UNCLE SAM
AN AMERICAN ICON

Retold by
JULIA McMEANS

Illustrated by
LORNA WILLIAM

Cavendish
Square
New York

A LONG TIME AGO, AN AMERICAN LEGEND WAS BORN. The legend was born before the Statue of Liberty was built. And before the Gateway Arch stretched over St. Louis. It was even born before there was a United States of America.

This legend wasn't like most other legends. It's not about a headless horseman or a ruthless train robber. Instead, it's the story of a simple man. His name was Samuel Wilson.

What's that? You say you've never heard of Samuel Wilson? Well, of course not! You probably know him better by his nickname. It was the name that made him famous, after all. Uncle Sam!

Now, legends are kind of strange things. You can't say they're one hundred percent true, but you can't say they're one hundred percent false either. Legends—even this one about old Uncle Sam—are a little bit of both.

Samuel Wilson was born in Arlington, Massachusetts, in September 1766. That was ten years before Thomas Jefferson wrote the Declaration of Independence. The declaration proclaimed that "all men are created equal"! Back then, there was no United States of America. There were just thirteen colonies. All thirteen colonies were ruled by an English king named George.

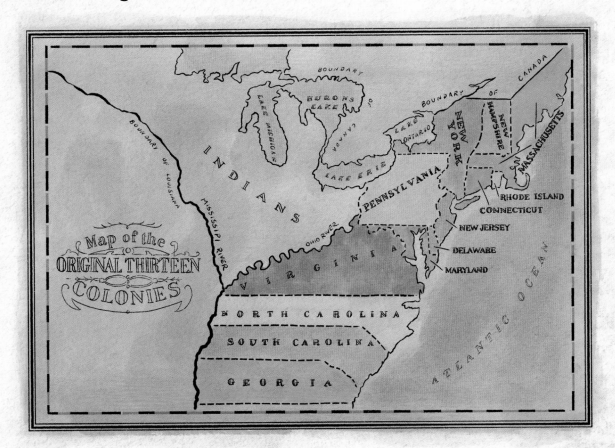

When Sam was a boy, his family moved from the Massachusetts Bay Colony to the colony of New Hampshire. They built a house in the town of Mason. By then, young Sam had a baby brother, named Ebenezer. The two of them became best friends.

Sam and Ebenezer probably spent their young days doing the same things that many colonial children did. Of course, they learned reading, writing, and arithmetic, but they played a lot too! And you might be surprised to learn that children back then played a lot of the same games that children play today. There was tag, hide-and-go-seek, leap frog, jump rope—well, I guess you could say that some things never get old! Of course, they played a few games that kids today don't play, like nine pins and rolling the hoop. Still looks like fun!

When Sam was twenty-two years old, he decided to leave Mason. He wanted to strike out on his own, find his own job, and live his own life. He wanted the same things most young folks do.

By now it was 1788, and America was its own country. General George Washington was president, and Americans were moving all across the United States.

And so was Sam. Sam walked 125 miles (201 kilometers) from Mason, New Hampshire, to Troy, New York. Troy was located along the Hudson River. It was a beautiful part of the country.

Back in Sam's day there were basically only three ways that people and goods could get around. They could get there on foot, on a horse, or on a boat, and for that last one, you needed water.

If you study a map of all the towns and cities in early America, you will find a river nearby. Rivers are good for transportation because they just flow one into another into another, until eventually they flow out to sea.

Sam was one of the first white pioneers to settle in the town of Troy. Up until then, Native Americans of the Mohican Nation had lived in the area. In fact, they had been living there for a long time.

Once Sam got settled, he got to work. His brother Ebenezer lived in the town too. Both he and Ebenezer had several different kinds of jobs and businesses there. For instance, Ebenezer was a justice of the peace. A justice of the peace is a judge who works in a small town. Rumor has it that Sam started the first brick-making company in the United States.

After a while, the brothers started the E & S Wilson meatpacking company. This company would eventually earn Sam his nickname.

In 1812, a war broke out between the United States and Great Britain. By now, James Madison, the author of the Bill of Rights, was president, and Sam was married to Betsey Mann.

The War of 1812, as the war was called, had a lot to do with international trade. That's when countries exchange goods with one another for money. Trade was just as important then as it is now. All of the international trade that happened back in Sam's time happened across the oceans.

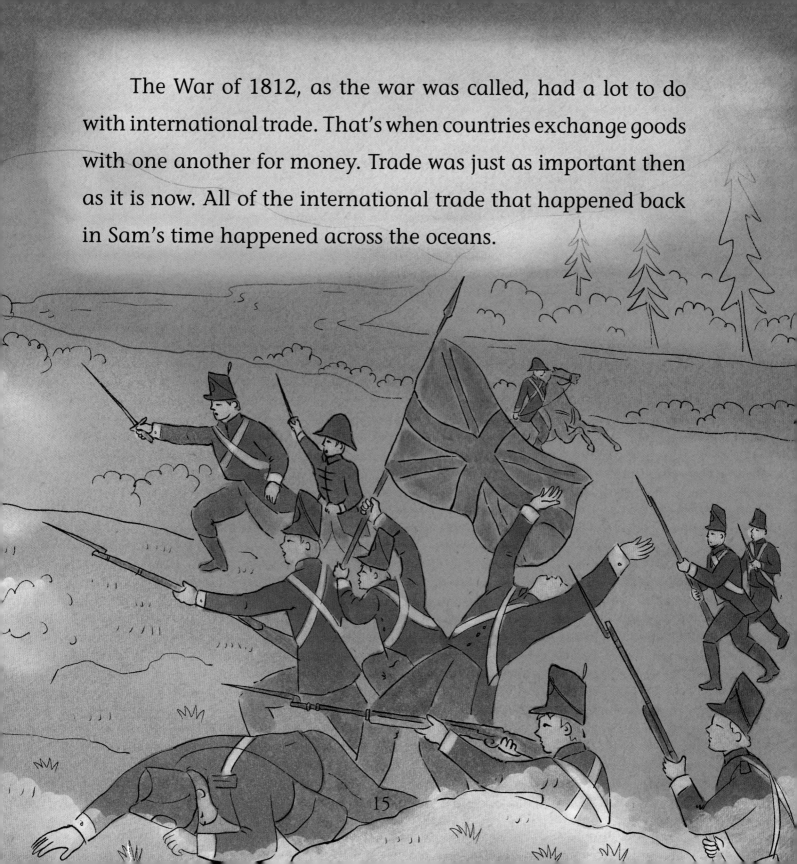

In the early 1800s, large ships crisscrossed the Atlantic Ocean. They carried cotton, coffee, lumber, fur—you name it—all over the world. These journeys were long and dangerous. It was important that ships share the ocean peacefully so they could safely deliver their cargo. But England and France, who had fought many wars with each other, were fighting again. And this time, the young United States got caught right in middle of it.

The problem was that the United States traded with Great Britain *and* France. But Great Britain got greedy and decided to block all US ships from entering French seaports. They insisted that American ships stop at a British port first and pay money before being allowed to continue. At that time, Great Britain had the most powerful navy in the world. They felt pretty sure that they could enforce this new rule.

But the British were also up to some other funny business. They captured American vessels on the seas and forced US sailors to join the British navy and fight the French! On the North American continent, they encouraged Native Americans to stop pioneers from moving west.

The War of 1812 was fought out on the ocean and within the United States. Battles were fought along the Atlantic coast and in New York State. In 1814, British soldiers invaded Washington, DC. They burned the White House and the Capitol building to the ground.

Back in Troy, business was booming for the E & S meatpacking company. One day, Sam and Ebenezer received an order for five thousand barrels of salted beef and pork. The barrels were stamped *US*. This meant they were to go to the United States Army. All the barrels traveled about 10 miles (16 km) down the Hudson River to the town of Greenbush, where the soldiers were stationed.

Since Troy and Greenbush are a short distance apart, quite a few soldiers knew about Sam Wilson and his meatpacking company. When they saw those barrels stamped *US*, they just started calling it "Uncle Sam's." Soon, Samuel Wilson just became known as good old Uncle Sam!

The War of 1812 eventually ended and America was once again victorious. Sam and Betsey Wilson had four children and lived out their days in Troy, New York.

Samuel Wilson, the lad who set out on foot in 1788 to make a name for himself, wound up with one of the most famous names in history. He died in 1854 at the age of eighty-eight. He was buried beside his beloved Betsey in Oakwood Cemetery in Troy, New York.

But Uncle Sam's legend lives on today! Over time, he has come to symbolize not only the government of the United States, but also love of country. It didn't happen right away, but slowly, year by year, images of Uncle Sam began to appear.

In 1917, the artist James Montgomery Flagg created the most well-known image of Uncle Sam. This Uncle Sam had white hair, bushy eyebrows, and a long white beard. He dressed in all red, white, and blue, and wore a top hat. The image was used during World War I as an army recruitment poster. That's where the famous *I Want You* slogan comes from.

In 1961, the United States Congress officially recognized Samuel Wilson as the person on whom the legend of Uncle Sam is based. They declared that Uncle Sam was the country's official symbol of strength and patriotism.

In 1989, President George H.W. Bush declared September 13 as Uncle Sam Day. It is the perfect day to remember him too. September 13 was the birthday of the real Samuel Wilson.

☆ SEPTEMBER ☆						
SUN	MON	TUE	WED	THU	FRI	SAT
					1	2
3	4	5	6	7	8	9
10	11	12	13	14	15	16
17	18	19	20	21	22	23
24	25	26	27	28	29	30

HAPPY BIRTHDAY!

ABOUT THE LEGEND

Like many legends, the origin of the Uncle Sam tale is not entirely known. This retelling is based on what has been officially recognized as the origination of the story. There are historical references to Uncle Sam, however, that have little to do with Samuel Wilson. In the 1950s, DC Comics created a superhero called Uncle Sam. This character was a member of the Justice League. In 1989, the city of Troy, New York, immortalized Uncle Sam by putting up a statue in his likeness.

WORDS TO KNOW

cargo The goods carried onboard a ship, plane, or train.

colony Land that is owned by another country but might be in a different part of the world.

international Between and among nations.

patriotism The love of your country.

pioneers The first people to settle a place.

slogan A group of words.

TO FIND OUT MORE

BOOKS

Isaacs, Sandy Senzell. *What Caused the War of 1812?* New York: Crabtree Publishing Company, 2011.

Saunders-Smith, Gail. *Uncle Sam.* North Mankato, MN: Capstone Press, 2013.

WEBSITES

Ducksters Education Site: US History: War of 1812

http://www.ducksters.com/history/us_1800s/war_of_1812.php

This website discusses the causes and consequences of the War of 1812.

A Walk Through the Uncle Sam House

https://www.youtube.com/watch?v=mHll5TdaKx8

This short video takes viewers on a walking tour of the Samuel Wilson house in Mason, New Hampshire.

ABOUT THE AUTHOR

Julia McMeans is an author and educator who has been writing for school students for over ten years. She is the author of many books, including *Differentiated Lessons and Assessments for Social Studies* and *Civic Values: Justice in Our Society*. McMeans also works extensively in museum education, both on the east and west coasts. She lives in La Jolla, California, with her husband and two chubby cats.

ABOUT THE ILLUSTRATOR

Lorna William grew up in rural Maine. She loved being in the woods and in the snow that covered them most of the time. Over the years she has raced bikes, raised children, fixed cars, and cleared fields. Currently, she is pursuing her passion for illustration.

Published in 2019 by Cavendish Square Publishing, LLC
243 5th Avenue, Suite 136, New York, NY 10016

Library of Congress Cataloging-in-Publication Data

Names: McMeans, Julia, author. | William, Lorna, illustrator.
Title: Uncle Sam : an American icon / Julia McMeans ; illustrated by Lorna William.
Description: First edition. | New York, NY : Cavendish Square Publishing, LLC, [2019] |
Series: American legends and folktales | Summary: "A retelling of the story of the iconic
Uncle Sam."--Provided by publisher. | Audience: Grades 3-5.
Identifiers: LCCN 2017051181 (print) | LCCN 2017053557 (ebook) | ISBN 9781502636980 (ebook) |
ISBN 9781502636973 (library bound) | ISBN 9781502636997 (pbk.) | ISBN 9781502637000 (6 pack)
Subjects: LCSH: Uncle Sam (Symbolic character)--Juvenile literature.
Classification: LCC E179 (ebook) | LCC E179 .M476 2019 (print) | DDC 398.22--dc23
LC record available at https://lccn.loc.gov/2017051181

Editorial Director: David McNamara
Editor: Kristen Susienka
Copy Editor: Alex Tessman
Associate Art Director: Amy Greenan
Designer: Alan Sliwinski
Illustrator: Lorna William
Production Coordinator: Karol Szymczuk

Printed in the United States of America